Elite Warriors

MARINE RAIDERS REGIMENT

JULIA GARSTECKI

BLACK RABBIT BOOKS

Bolt is published by Black Rabbit Books
P.O. Box 227, Mankato, Minnesota, 56002.
www.blackrabbitbooks.com

Marysa Storm, editor; Grant Gould & Michael Sellner, designers; Omay Ayres, photo researcher

Library of Congress Cataloging-in-Publication Data
Names: Garstecki, Julia, author.
Title: Marine Raiders Regiment / by Julia Garstecki.
Description: Mankato, Minnesota : Black Rabbit Books, [2019] | Series: Bolt. Elite warriors | Includes bibliographical references and index. | Audience: Grades 4-6. | Audience: Ages 9-12.
Identifiers: LCCN 2017027575 (print) | LCCN 2017027791 (ebook) | ISBN 9781680725452 (ebook) | ISBN 9781680724295 (library binding) | ISBN 9781680727234 (paperback)
Subjects: LCSH: United States. Marine Corps–Commando troops–Juvenile literature. | United States. Marine Special Operations Command–Juvenile literature. Classification: LCC VE23 (ebook) | LCC VE23 .G376 2019 (print) | DDC 359.9/631–dc23
LC record available at https://lccn.loc.gov/2017027575

Printed in the United States.

Image Credits

Alamy: PJF Military Collection, 4–5, 9; US Marines Photo, 7; americanspecialops.com: US Marine Corps, 24 (top); archive.defense.gov: US Marine Corps/Cpl. Carson A. Gramley, 26–27; commons.wikimedia.org: US Marine Corps/Lance Cpl. Brian Bekkala, 22; US Marine Corps/Sgt. Brian A. Tuthill, 28; Dreamstime: Oleg Zabielin, Cover, 6, 18–19; dodlive.mil: US Marine Corps/Cpl. Austin Long, 10; fsoc.af.mil: US Air Force/Senior Airman Ryan Conroy: 22–23, 23; marinecorpstimes.com: US Marine Corps/Cpl. Olivia McDonald, 13 (top); marsoc.marines.mil: US Marine Corps, 21 (middle, bttm), 24 (bttm); US Marine Corps/Master Sgt. Jeremiah Erickson, 13 (bttm); US Marine Corps/Cpl. Richard Blumenstein, 21 (top); US Marine Corps/Senior Airman Ryan Conroy, 16 (top); Shutterstock: Anatoly Vartanov, 16 (rifle); ARTYuSTUDIO, 18 (goggles); Boonchuay1970, 16 (pistol); Getmilitaryphotos, 3, 32; Ivan Cholakov, 14–15 (bkgd), 31; Maxim Apryatin, 1; Tony El-Azzi, 16 (knife); sanua9, 8 (camo); Yanas, 8 (metal)
Every effort has been made to contact copyright holders for material reproduced in this book. Any omissions will be rectified in subsequent printings if notice is given to the publisher.

CONTENTS

CHAPTER 1

In ACTION

In the late 2000s, **terrorists** controlled land in the country of Afghanistan. There, they planned attacks and trained fighters. The United States wanted to stop them. It sent Marine Raiders to the area.

Mission Accomplished

The Raiders worked with Afghan soldiers. Together, they fought the terrorists. Many lives were lost. But the soldiers forced their enemies from the area.

Who Are the Marine Raiders?

Marine Raiders make up the Marine Raider Regiment. It's part of the Marine Corps Forces Special Operations Command (MARSOC). Raiders are highly trained Marines. They go on short **missions** to dangerous places. They work in small groups. But their actions have big results.

MARSOC formed in 2006. It's one of the youngest U.S. special ops forces.

CHAPTER 2

Many Jobs, MANY PLACES

Raiders capture or take down enemies. They often work with other groups of U.S. soldiers. Together, they fight people who want to harm the United States. They make the world a safer place.

"Always Faithful, Always Forward" is a MARSOC saying.

Training and Teaching

Raiders don't just help U.S. soldiers. They help forces from other countries too. They train them to fight. To do so, Raiders must speak different languages. They need to understand other **cultures**.

WHERE RAIDERS HAVE WORKED

Raiders work around the world. Their missions are kept secret. But people know Raiders have given support in the following regions.

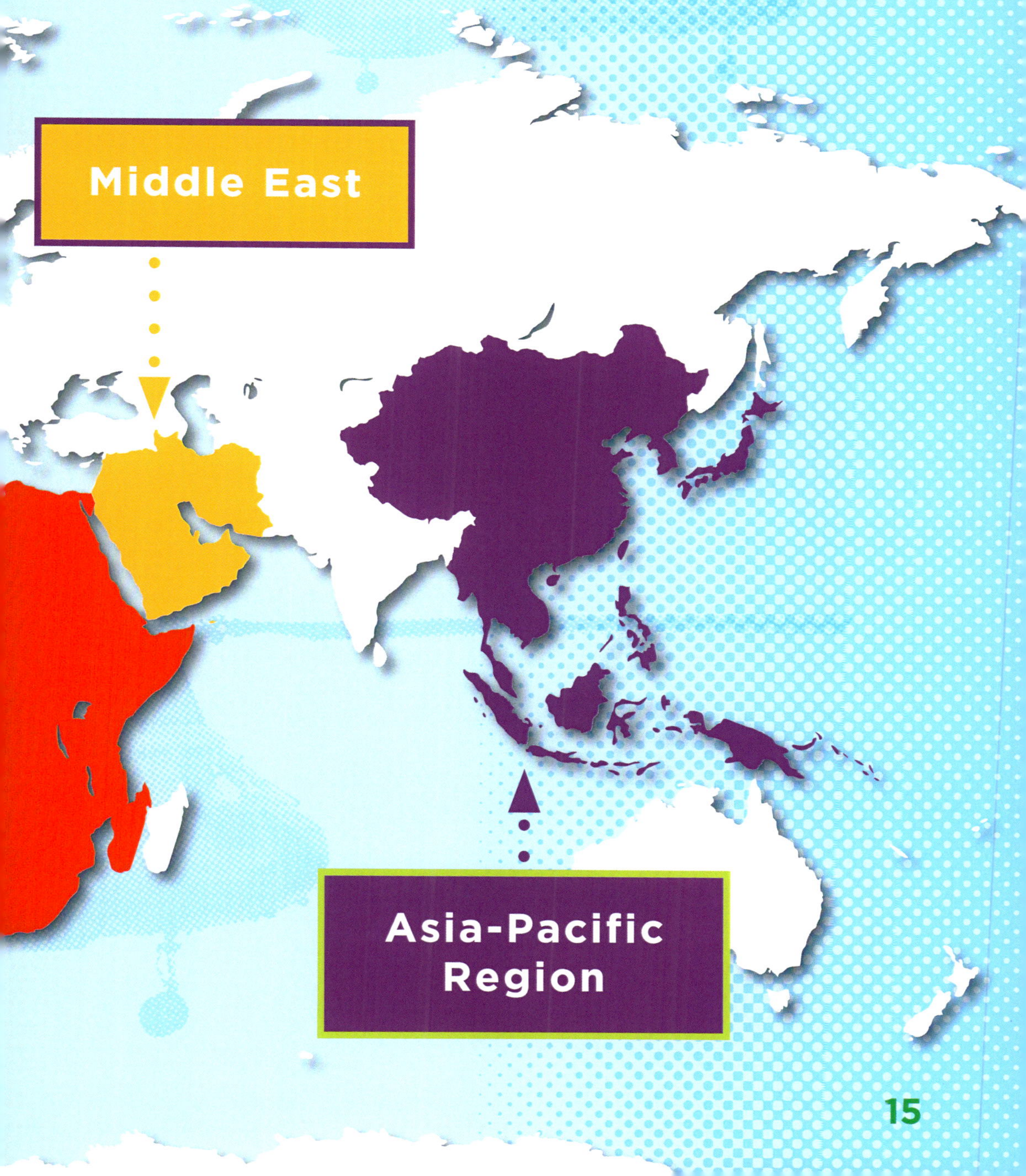
Middle East
Asia-Pacific Region

Raiders' Weapons

rifle

pistol

knife

CHAPTER 3

WEAPONS and Gear

Raiders need weapons. They use Glock 19 pistols. Parts for the gun can be found around the world. Because Raiders travel, being able to get parts is important.

Raiders also use many tools. Being able to speak different languages is one of them.

ALWAYS PREPARED

GLOVES
NIGHT-VISION GOGGLES
BOOTS

CHAPTER 4

TOUGH Training

Joining MARSOC is hard work. **Recruits** must first pass selection phases. The phases test soldiers' physical fitness. Soldiers perform many tough exercises. Marines must be more than just strong, though. They must also be great leaders.

569
830

94

SWIMMING DURING SELECTION AND ASSESSMENT

Raiders must be good swimmers. Recruits do many exercises in water.

4 MINUTES

how long Marines must perform a survival float

20 FEET

(6 METERS) PLATFORM HEIGHT MARINES JUMP FROM DURING ABANDON-SHIP DRILL

HOW FAR MARINES MUST SWIM IN UNIFORM

984 FEET
(300 M)

11 MINUTES
how long Marines must tread water

Phases One and Two

Passing the selection phases is just the beginning. The Individual Training Course comes next.

The first phase of the course lasts 10 weeks. Recruits spend a lot of time swimming. They also practice fighting. Recruits develop survival skills too.

During phase two, Marines learn to gather information. Soldiers also work with small boats. This stage lasts eight weeks.

Phases Three and Four

The third phase of the training course lasts five weeks. Soldiers practice **raids**. They also spend hours shooting weapons. Raiders must have excellent aim.

The last phase takes seven weeks. Recruits put everything they have learned to the test. After passing this phase, they're officially Raiders. They're ready to go on missions.

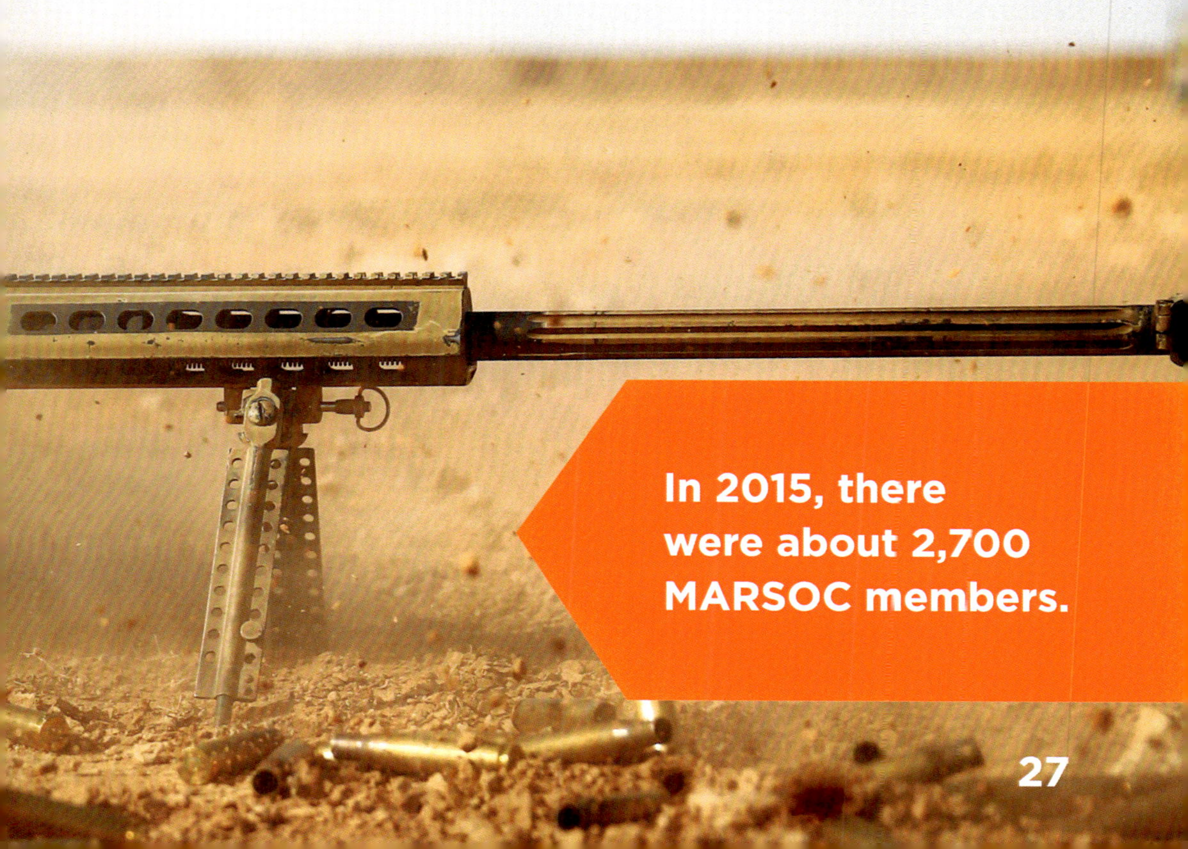

In 2015, there were about 2,700 MARSOC members.

Always Ready

Raiders are more than tough soldiers. They must make good decisions in difficult situations. These elite warriors are always ready for missions.

GLOSSARY

culture (KUHL-cher)—the habits, beliefs, and traditions of a particular people, place, or time

mission (MISH-uhn)—a job assigned to a soldier

pistol (PIS-tl)—a small gun whose chamber is part of the barrel

raid (REYD)—a surprise attack on an enemy by soldiers

recruit (ri-KROOT)—a newcomer to a group or field of activity

region (REE-juhn)—a part of a country or the world that is different or separate from other parts in some way

rifle (RI-ful)—a shoulder weapon with grooves in the barrels

terrorist (TER-ur-ist)—a person who uses violent acts to frighten people in order to achieve a goal

LEARN MORE

BOOKS

Mitchell, P. P. *Join the Marines.* US Armed Forces. New York: Gareth Stevens Publishing, 2018.

Noll, Elizabeth. *Special Ops Forces.* Rank It! Mankato, MN: Black Rabbit Books, 2017.

Whiting, Jim. *Marine Corps Forces Special Operations Command.* U.S. Special Forces. Mankato, MN: Creative Education, 2015.

WEBSITES

Marine Raider Regiment
www.marsoc.marines.mil/Units/Marine-Raider-Regiment/

MARSOC Recruiting
marsoc.com

What It Takes to Be a MARSOC Marine Raider
www.youtube.com/watch?v=ldL1Lr1DVBY

INDEX